7/14 3-2 ᴜᴛᴅ 7/14

Dragon Slayers' Academy™

BEWARE!
IT'S FRIDAY THE 13TH

By Kate McMullan

Illustrated by Bill Basso

GROSSET & DUNLAP

Visit us at www.abdopublishing.com

Spotlight, a division of ABDO Publishing Company, is a distributor of high quality reinforced library bound editions for schools and libraries.

This library bound edition is published by arrangement with Penguin Young Readers Group, a member of Penguin Group (USA) Inc.

For everyone at Paul J. Bellew Elementary
West Islip, New York,
especially Kimberly, who said
Friday the 13th—K. McM.

To Marie and Luca—B. B.

Library of Congress Cataloging-in-Publication Data

McMullan, Kate.
  Beware! It's Friday the 13th / by Kate McMullan ; illustrated by Bill Basso.
    p. cm. – (Dragon Slayers' Academy)
  Beware! It is Friday the 13th
  Beware! It is Friday the thirteenth
  Summary: Upon superstitious headmaster Mordred's orders, the returning students and new lasses of Dragon Slayers' Academy deck themselves in lucky charms on Friday the thirteenth, but luck may not help when a wicked dragon arrives seeking revenge.
  ISBN-13: 978-1-59961-122-8 (reinforced library bound edition)
  ISBN-10: 1-59961-122-8 (reinforced library bound edition)
  [1. Dragons—Fiction. 2. Schools—Fiction. 3. Superstition—Fiction.] I. Basso, Bill, ill. II. Title. III. Title: Beware! It is Friday the 13th. IV. Title: Beware! It is Friday the thirteenth. V. Series: McMullan, Kate. Dragon Slayers' Academy.

PZ7.M47879Be 2006
[Fic]—dc22   2006013400

Chapter I

"**Z**ounds!" exclaimed Wiglaf as he ran out of the Dragon Slayers' Academy castle. "We're going to have a school picnic!"

In the yard, blue-and-white DSA flags flapped in the morning breeze. Brightly colored picnic cloths dotted the grass. A long banner stretched across the yard saying:

WELCOME TO DSA, LASSES!

"This is so cool!" exclaimed Janice. "At Dragon Whackers, we never had a school picnic." She blew a big green bubble of Smilin' Hal's Tree Sap Gum.

Janice Smotherbottom was DSA's newest student. After she came, Mordred decided to open DSA's doors to all lasses.

"I cannot wait until the new lasses get here!" Erica said.

Erica had gone to DSA for some time. But until recently, she pretended to be a lad. Mordred never guessed that "Eric" was a lass—*and* a princess.

"The new lasses shall need a good example," Erica went on. "Someone to show them what to do." She patted the Future Dragon Slayer of the Month Medal hanging from a chain around her neck. "And I am the perfect one to show them how to do *everything*!"

"Look over there!" said Angus, who was plump and fond of food. He pointed to a long table heaped with meat pies, breads, cheeses, and bowls of apples.

Wiglaf's stomach growled softly at the sight of so much good food. Breakfast that morning had been leftover eel. He had not been able to choke down much of it.

"It's a feast!" Angus exclaimed.

"Indeed it is," said Mordred's sister Lady Lobelia as she stepped out of the castle. She wore a blue gown with a spray of yellow feathers at the throat. "Mordie spent a pretty penny on it, too. Yet he is sure to get his gold back ten times over when all the new lasses pay their tuition."

Lobelia cupped her hands to her mouth. "Class I!" she called. "Come! Quickly!"

Class I gathered by Lady Lobelia. Wiglaf and his friends joined them.

"The Class II and III lads are still off in the Dark Forest collecting stones for building the new dorm," Lobelia said.

"A dorm for us lasses!" exclaimed Janice.

Lobelia smiled. "So it is up to you, Class I, to show the new lasses the true DSA spirit!"

Erica raised her hand. "May we welcome them with the DSA cheer?"

"Oh, yes! Do!" exclaimed Lady Lobelia.

"You shall each get—" She stopped. "Janice, are you chewing gum?"

Janice stopped chewing and swallowed. "Not anymore."

Lobelia rolled her eyes. "You shall each pick a lass to be your buddy," she went on. "First take your buddy to meet her teachers. Then take her over to Frypot's feast table and help her fill her plate. Then sit with her at the picnic."

"Oh, yummy!" cried Angus.

"The feast is for the new lasses, Angus," warned Lobelia.

"No!" cried Angus. "You can't mean—"

"I do," said Lobelia. "Frypot will give each of you old students a delicious box lunch of chopped eel on a toasted loaf."

A chorus of groans sounded.

"I don't mind!" called Janice. "I'm growing to like eel!"

"Now I have a surprise!" said Lobelia

brightly. "Erica and Janice? Come into the castle with me. We'll be right back, lads!"

Erica and Janice followed Lobelia eagerly up the steps and into the castle.

"I shall pick a tiny lass for my buddy," Angus said after they left. "One who does not eat much. One who likes to share her food."

In a short time, Lady Lobelia was back.

"Preeeeee-senting!" she cried. "DSA's new Lobelia Original lasses' uniform!" She turned toward the castle. "Models! Appear!"

Erica and Janice stepped out of the castle.

Wiglaf gasped. "Oh, poor Erica!" he said to Angus. "Poor Janice!"

Erica and Janice stood before Class I wearing plum-colored tops that laced up the front and tied under the chin with a floppy bow. Their hands stuck out from huge, puffy plum sleeves. The matching plum skirts were fringed at the hem with tiny silver bells. Their helmets bulged out at the sides, then came to

a point at the top.

"Here's the best part!" said Lobelia. "You lasses are going to model this uniform tomorrow at the Toenail Fashion Show!"

Janice laughed and twirled around. But Erica stood frowning with her puffy-sleeved arms folded across her chest.

"We are lucky to be lads!" Wiglaf whispered.

Angus nodded. "That uniform makes Janice look like a great big plum pudding."

"Excuse me, Lady Lobelia?" Erica said. "How can we sneak up on a dragon while wearing *bells?*" She took a step and clinked merrily.

"Don't they make a lovely tinkle?" Lobelia said, missing Erica's point entirely.

"One more thing," Lobelia said in a voice hardly more than a whisper. "Your headmaster is a happy man today. And we don't want to spoil his good mood. So when you see Mordred, whatever you do, do not mention what day it is."

"What day is it?" asked Janice.

Lobelia whispered, "Friday the 13th."

"Friday the 13th?" cried Torblad, who was afraid of everything. "Egad! Unlucky day!"

"Shhhhhh!" Lobelia put a finger to her lips. "Do not say that aloud! If Mordred hears you..." She closed her eyes and shook her head. "We shall all be very, very sorry."

Chapter 2

"This is so not fair," said Erica. "This uniform is ridiculous!" She took off her pointy helmet and tossed it to the ground.

"Angus?" said Janice. "Why can't your uncle Mordred know it's Friday the 13th?"

Angus shrugged. "Auntie Lobelia always keeps it a secret from him. That's all I know."

"Maybe he is superstitious, like my father," said Wiglaf. "If my father hears a dog howl in the night, he stays in bed all the next day. He never takes a bath, for he says bathing causes madness. And he often rings a bell to drive away demons."

"Does that work?" asked Torblad eagerly.

"It must," said Wiglaf. "For no demon has

ever come to our hovel."

"Fiddle-faddle," said Erica. "I do not believe in superstitions."

Just then—TWEEEEEEEET! The headmaster's whistle tooted.

Wiglaf turned to see Mordred standing on the castle steps. He was decked out like a king—in a purple cape trimmed in gold braid. His gold rings sparkled in the morning sun.

Lobelia stood beside her brother, holding a large scroll. Wiglaf had signed his name on that scroll. Every DSA student had.

"Good morning, all!" boomed Mordred.

"Good morning, Headmaster!" the Class I lads and lasses sang out.

"What a good plan, letting lasses into DSA!" Mordred exclaimed. "I cannot wait to sign them up. More students—more tuition!" He grinned, and his gold tooth gleamed. "Why, this day shall go down in history!" He frowned. "What day is it, anyway?"

Torblad called out, "It's Friday the—"

Angus quickly elbowed him.

"Ow!" cried Torblad.

"It is the feast day of St. Helga's Handkerchief," Erica called out.

"Also the feast day of St. Albert's Anklebone!" called Wiglaf.

"Here comes your chair, Mordie," Lobelia said quickly to distract her brother. "Where do you want it?"

"In the shade there." Mordred waved a gold-ringed hand toward the castle wall.

Two student teachers struggled down the steps with the heavy, throne-like chair.

The headmaster turned back to Class I. TWEEEEEEEEET! He blew his whistle. "To the gatehouse, laggards!" he bellowed. "Stand by to welcome the new lasses!"

Wiglaf and his friends started off. On the way to the gatehouse, they met Brother Dave, the DSA librarian, coming from the South

Tower. He wore his brown monk's robe, tied round the middle with a length of rope. Today he had a basket over one arm.

"Good morn to thee, lads and lasses," Brother Dave said. He was ever cheerful, though it was not easy being the librarian at DSA, where only three of the students and none of the teachers had ever read a whole book. Those three students lingered behind as their classmates went on to the gatehouse.

"Erica," said Brother Dave, "art thou still reading *All About Sir Lancelot*?"

"For the sixteenth time," said Erica. "May I renew it?"

"Certainly." The little monk smiled.

"Brother Dave?" said Angus. "Breakfast this morning was awful. Do you happen to have any brittle in your basket?"

"I bringeth it as a treat for the new lasses," said the monk. His order, Little Brothers of the Peanut Brittle, was famous for making sweet peanut candy. "But there is plenty for thee, too." He reached into his basket and broke off bits of brittle. Wiglaf and Angus took theirs eagerly.

"No, thanks," said Erica. "I never eat between meals."

Angus bit in and said, "Mmmmm!"

Wiglaf did the same. "You are the best brittle baker, Brother Dave," he said.

"No, no," said Brother Dave. "My Little Brothers back at the monastery sendeth me this brittle. For I cannot baketh a fine sticky brittle. Mine turneth out hard as a rock."

Brother Dave looked so sad that Wiglaf thought it best to change the subject.

"Has Worm come back yet, Brother Dave?" he asked.

Worm was a young dragon. Wiglaf and Angus had snuck his dragon egg into the Class I dorm, where he had hatched. Now he lived part-time up in the DSA library, flying in and out through its wide windows at will. Brother Dave was the only teacher who knew about Worm.

The monk shook his head. "Worm stayeth still in the Dark Forest with his dragon family," he said.

"He has been gone a fortnight," Wiglaf said. "I fear he has forgotten us."

"No, no, my fine lads," Brother Dave said. "He couldst never forget thee!"

A sudden blast of trumpets sounded outside the castle wall. Wiglaf heard the clip-clop of horses' hooves on the drawbridge. He, Angus, and Erica ran to the gatehouse.

The gates swung open. Pairs of white horses pulled two golden carriages into the castle yard. Several lasses stepped down from each carriage. Last through the gate came a small lass riding a fine red pony. She wore a red gown and red slippers. A fancy red-and-white bag hung over her shoulder. Her hair

was the color of ripe red apples.

Never in all Wiglaf's days had he seen anyone with such bright red hair. It made his own carrot-colored hair seem almost pale.

The red-haired lass jumped down from her pony and sent it trotting off to the stables. The other lasses gathered around her.

"I once knew a lass with red hair like hers," Erica whispered as the empty carriages turned around and left DSA. "But this cannot be she. That lass loved playing dress-up and having tea parties. She would never come to a dragon-slaying school."

Erica turned to Class I. "All right!" she shouted. "Let's welcome the new lasses!"

Together they cheered:

"Rooty-toot-ho! Rooty-toot-hey!
We're Class I from DSA!
We stalk dragons, yes we do!
Big ones! Bony ones! Fat ones, too!

We stalk dragons, young and old!
We slay dragons, grab their gold!
Yay! Yay! For good old DSA—hey!"

"That is so cute!" said the redheaded lass. "Oh, I just know I'm going to love it here!"

Erica's eyes grew wide. "St. Dominic's dog!" she exclaimed. "Is that Gwendolyn?"

Chapter 3

"Welcome, lasses!" Mordred called. "I am Mordred de Marvelous, Headmaster of Dragon Slayers' Academy." He galloped toward the gate, his purple cape billowing out behind. "And you are—"

"Princesses!" announced the redheaded lass.

"Never interrupt *me*!" Mordred snapped. Then one of his bushy eyebrows arched way up. "Did you say...princesses?"

"One and all," said Gwendolyn. "I am Princess Gwendolyn of Gargglethorp."

"Oh, woe is us!" Erica shook her head, but it made her bells jingle, so she stopped.

"Gargglethorp?" Mordred squeaked. "That is a big kingdom. Very big. And very rich."

"Very," said Gwendolyn. "We all went to Princess Prep. Now we want to go to DSA."

The other princesses nodded.

"So you shall!" Mordred sped to his throne-like chair and sat down. "Come! Fork over your...I mean, I shall sign you up and collect your tuition." He unrolled his scroll.

The princesses scampered over to him.

Gwen stepped up first. "How much, Headmaster?" she asked.

"Sev—" Mordred stopped. He narrowed his eyes. "I mean...ten pennies."

Wiglaf gasped. DSA tuition had always been seven pennies. Angus's mom had paid his seven. But *ten* pennies? That was a fortune!

Gwen began emptying her fancy red-and-white bag. Wiglaf watched, amazed, as she pulled out a fancy gold brush and comb, jewel-studded barrettes, a silver looking glass, an eyelash curler, nail gloss, a couple of magazines, a newspaper, and finally a red-velvet coin purse.

"Ten pennies is all?" she asked. "Princess Prep cost far more than ten pennies."

"Not ten," Mordred said quickly. "Ten-tee, TEN-tee, twwwwenty pennies." He held out his hand once more.

"Uncle Mordred is shameless," Angus whispered.

Gwendolyn dropped twenty pennies into Mordred's waiting palm.

Wiglaf had never seen so many pennies at one time in his life!

Mordred bit each one to make sure it was real. Then he put the pennies into the purse he wore strapped across his chest.

"Sign here," he said, pointing to the scroll.

She signed "Gwendolyn," making the *o* in the shape of a heart.

"Welcome to DSA!" said Mordred. "Now

step aside. Shoo!" He waggled a finger at the princess in line behind Gwen. "Next!"

As the other princesses were signing up, Gwen began stuffing her things back into her bag. "Now what?" she asked.

"Now you shall get a DSA buddy," said Lobelia, coming over to them. "Who wants to be Princess Gwendolyn's buddy?"

Many Class I hands went up.

"Let me see..." said Lobelia. "I think..."

"I'll pick," said Gwendolyn firmly.

The castle yard grew still as the princess walked down the row of Class I lads and lasses, looking them over.

Baldrick wiped his runny nose with the back of his hand. "Pick me," he said. "I've been in Class I the longest."

"I'm from Toenail! That's right near Gargglethorp!" cried Torblad. "Pick me!"

Gwendolyn kept going. She stopped

suddenly. "Erica von Royale? From Pretty Little Princess Preschool? Is it really *you*?"

Erica nodded. "Hello, Gwen."

Wiglaf grinned. "Pretty Little Princess Preschool?"

"I was only three," Erica muttered. "My parents made me go." She looked at Gwen. "I am much surprised that you wish to study dragon slaying."

Gwen shrugged. "I am sick of going to a princess school. I have learned the Princess Walk. And the Princess Smile. Now I'm ready to meet boys. To have adventures!"

"You've come to the right school!" said Janice. "So much happens here! A couple weeks ago? There was this ghost—"

"Thank you, Janice!" Lobelia cut her off. She turned to Gwen. "Would you like Erica to be your DSA buddy, dear?"

"Yes," said Gwendolyn. "And him." She

pointed to Angus. "And the cute one with the carroty hair."

Cute? Wiglaf felt his face grow warm.

"One buddy per lass," said Lobelia.

Gwen favored Lady Lobelia with a dazzling smile. "I always like to have more of everything than anyone else," she said.

"Oh, my dear!" exclaimed Lobelia. "You really are a princess!"

"What am I, chopped eel liver?" muttered Erica. She glared at Gwen.

"Buddies!" chirped Lobelia. "Take the princess over to meet her teachers."

"Wait, Lady Lobelia!" said Erica. "First I must ask the new lasses a most important question."

Everyone moved closer to hear Erica's question. Even Mordred, weighed down by his bulging purse of pennies, lumbered over to hear what Erica had to say.

Erica began turning around. She jingled

softly. "What do you think of this new uniform?"

Wiglaf could tell she thought that they would all hate it.

Gwen kept her eyes fastened on Erica until she had turned all the way around. Then she ran up to her and straightened the floppy bow under her chin. She stepped back to study the change.

The other princesses looked to Gwen to speak for them.

"I, personally, would never wear the helmet," said Gwen at last.

Lady Lobelia gasped.

Erica grinned.

"But the rest of the uniform," said Gwen, "is fabulous."

"*What?*" cried Erica.

"Yes!" exclaimed Lobelia. "That is the very word I use to describe it myself!"

"Are you jesting, Gwen?" cried Erica.

Gwen put her hands on her hips. "You never did have an eye for fashion, Erica," she said. "Even at Pretty Little Princess Preschool. You never came near the dress-up corner. You were always outside in that filthy sandbox."

"I was making a scale model of Sir Lancelot's castle at Camelot out of *sand*!" Erica cried.

Wiglaf had never seen her so upset.

Gwen only shrugged. She pointed to Erica's puffy sleeves. "These say strength with softness," she said. "The bells are pure genius. And the color?" She dumped out the contents of her bag again. She grabbed the newspaper. It was *Damsels' Wear Daily*. She flipped through the pages until she found what she was looking for. She read: " 'This year's big color is—plum!' "

"Oh!" Lady Lobelia clasped her hands to her chest. "I wonder if *Damsels' Wear Daily* would do a piece on Lobelia Originals."

"I can't wait to put on my uniform," said Gwen. She began tossing her things back into her bag.

Now Mordred said, "Let me see that paper of yours."

Gwen handed it to him.

"Mordie!" shrieked Lobelia. "This is no time to read the paper! Go—go count your pennies!"

"Hush, sister." Mordred waved her away. "I took out an ad in *Damsels' Wear Daily* saying that lasses are welcome at DSA. I want to see if it ran."

"No, Uncle!" Angus ran over and snatched the paper from his uncle's hands. "It's uh—time for the picnic!"

Mordred grabbed it back and stared at the front page.

The castle yard grew still.

Mordred did not move a muscle. He was as still as a stone statue. Then his purple eyes began to bulge.

"I think Uncle Mordred just found out

that it's Friday the 13th," said Angus.

The headmaster's mouth opened and shut. No sound came out.

"Alas and alack!" cried Lobelia.

The newspaper fell from Mordred's hand. He let out a blood-chilling yell, jumped up, and ran screaming into the castle.

Chapter 4

"Princesses!" Lady Lobelia called. "Worry not! Your headmaster has a headache. He'll be fine." She smiled a shaky smile. "Come! I shall give you your DSA uniforms!"

The princesses ran off to the castle.

Wiglaf spied the *Damsels' Wear Daily* that Mordred had dropped. He picked it up to give it back to Gwen.

"Let us see what sort of silly paper Gwen carries around," said Erica.

Wiglaf was curious too. Together, they read:

DAMSELS' WEAR DAILY
FRIDAY, THE XIIITH
TOENAIL FASHION SHOW CANCELED!
Dragon Seen Heading for DSA

Wiglaf and Erica stared at the headline.

"Let me see that," said Angus. He read the headline. "Aaaaaaaaaaaaaahhhhh!" he screamed. "A dragon is coming here!"

Brother Dave and the other teachers hurried over. The Class I lads did too. The princesses ran out of the castle, filling the air with a near-deafening tinkling of bells.

"Who screamed?" said Gwen. "What's wrong?"

Wiglaf tried to hold the paper steady in his trembling hands so that all might read:

TOENAIL VILLAGE—Friday

Verbosia Vanity, the best-dressed damsel in Toenail, has canceled tomorrow's big fashion show. She spoke to the press wearing a plum-colored gown.

"It was a difficult decision," Verbosia told us. "The runway is ready. The models are here. The

designers have put the finishing touches on their outfits. Everyone in Toenail has bought a ticket to the event.

"But reports from far and wide say that Snagglefahng is headed this way. He's been stopping villagers and asking directions to Dragon Slayers' Academy, which is just south of our fair village. Word is that Snagglefahng is out to seek revenge."

She shook her head. "Snagglefahng is famous for torching villages for fun. We just can't take a chance on all those fabulous clothes going up in flames. The models, either," she added. "But just as soon as that dragon leaves DSA, we'll set a new date. The Toenail Fashion Show must go on!"

"A wicked dragon is coming to DSA?" Gwen shivered. To Wiglaf's dismay, she moved closer to him.

"See, Gwen? What did I tell you?" Janice

exclaimed happily. "There's always gobs of stuff happening around here!"

"But who could Snagglefahng be looking for here?" Erica wondered out loud.

"For me," Brother Dave whispered. The color had drained from his face. "Snagglefahng hath tracked me down at last."

"*You*, Brother Dave?" exclaimed Wiglaf.

"Whoa, Bro!" exclaimed Janice. "Why would a dragon be stalking you?"

"'Tis a long story," said Brother Dave. Then he took off toward the South Tower.

"What can he mean?" asked Wiglaf.

"Search me," said Erica. "Who's *that*?"

She had turned and was pointing to a large figure on the castle steps. Whoever it was wore a lacy cap tied under the chin. And a short, leopard-print tunic that left his hairy legs and one hairy shoulder bare. He wore old, holey boots. Something that looked very

like an eel hung around the person's neck.

TWEEEEEEEEET! A whistle sounded.

"Egad!" cried Angus. "Uncle Mordred?"

"Whoopie!" Janice cried out. "Dragon Whackers was never this wacky!"

"Neither was Princess Prep," muttered Gwen. "Ever."

"Today," boomed Mordred, "is Friday the 13th. Unlucky day! Unlucky day! Oh, woe!"

Lobelia joined Class I at the foot of the castle steps. When she saw her brother, she dabbed at her eyes with her hanky. "Oh, this is the worst he's ever been!"

"Is he ill?" asked Wiglaf.

"Yes," sniffled Lobelia. "Mordie has triskaidekaphobia."

"Does—does it run in our family, Auntie?" asked Angus.

"Is it catching?" asked Erica.

"'Tis the plague!" cried Torblad.

"No, it's not the plague," snapped Lobelia. "Triskaidekaphobia only means 'fear of Friday the 13th.' And Mordie's got a whopper of a case. Just look at him!"

"Unlucky day!" cried Mordred over and over. "Unlucky day!"

Lobelia shouted, "Mordie, stop!"

"Unlucky da—huh?" Mordred stared at Lobelia. "A wicked dragon is headed to my school, sister!" he cried. "Unlucky us!"

"Oh, piffle, Mordie!" said Lobelia. "You know how to turn bad luck to good!"

"I do?" Mordred seemed puzzled.

"Of course you do," said Lobelia. "All it takes is a few good-luck charms!"

"Ah, yes!" cried Mordred. "I am wearing good-luck charms. See? I have on my lucky bonnet. My lucky booties. My lucky wrestling suit."

"So that's what it is," said Erica.

"Around my neck," Mordred went on, "I'm wearing an eel—a lucky fish known to ward off evil! Ward off evil! Ward off—"

"Mordie!" yelled Lobelia. "Button it up!"

Mordred blinked. "Students!" he cried. "I have prepared for such an unlucky day!" He picked up a box at his feet. "In here, I have a lucky bonnet for each of you!"

"Hooray!" cried Torblad again.

"He's joking, right?" asked Gwen.

"I fear not," Lobelia said, and she began to weep in earnest.

On Mordred's orders, Frypot began handing out the lucky bonnets.

Wiglaf felt foolish as he tied his on. Yet if it would help to keep the wicked dragon away from Brother Dave, he would wear his lucky bonnet forever!

"One for you," said Frypot. He offered a bonnet to Princess Gwen.

"No, thank you," said Gwen.

"Not a choice, really," said Frypot. "On with it."

Gwen folded her arms across her chest.

"What's wrong, Gwen?" Erica said, putting on a lacy white cap. "Don't you think these bonnets are *fabulous*?"

Gwen grabbed a bonnet from Frypot. She put it on but did not tie the laces.

"You!" Mordred pointed to Torblad and Baldrick. "Go to the stable. Get horseshoes. Lucky horseshoes! Nail them to the castle."

The lads ran off.

"Nephew!" Mordred yelled. "You and Wiglaf. Go empty Frypot's eel traps. Get an eel for everyone!" He handed them a sack.

"You mean *we* have to—" Angus began.

"Go!" bellowed Mordred. "Lasses! Go to the field and find four-leaf clovers."

"Such are very rare, sir," said Erica.

"Find them!" Mordred bellowed. "Pin them on your lucky bonnets, on your uniforms. That will keep the dragon away. What are you waiting for? Go! Go! GO!"

Chapter 5

ncle Mordred always gives me the worst jobs!" wailed Angus as they hurried to the moat.

"Me too," said Wiglaf. "Angus, why would a dragon want to track down Brother Dave? He is a very kind monk. I'm sure he has never harmed any dragon."

Angus only shrugged. "Grab that rope," he said. "One, two, three—pull!"

The lads spent hours hauling up wooden traps filled with writhing black eels. After they emptied the last one, they trudged back to the castle yard, dragging their sack of eels behind them.

Baldrick and Torblad were busy nailing lucky horseshoes all along the castle wall.

The lads dragged their fishy cargo past the lasses, who were already back from the clover field.

"Zounds!" said Wiglaf. "Look how many four-leaf clovers the lasses found. They have them pinned all over their bonnets and uniforms!"

"Erica isn't wearing any," said Angus.

Wiglaf saw that this was true. They hurried over to her.

"What is wrong?" Wiglaf asked.

"You see every lass wearing four-leaf clovers," Erica said. "Yet we found none."

"None?" said Wiglaf, confused.

"Nah," said Janice, who, for once, wasn't chewing gum. "But Gwen had a clever idea. She's cool."

Wiglaf took a closer look at Janice's clovers.

"Why, these are three-leaf clovers!" he

exclaimed. "An extra leaf is stuck on with...gum?"

"Right!" Janice grinned. "I had to chew every piece in my pockets to get enough to stick all these clovers together."

"We had to do something, Wiglaf," said Gwen. "Or we would have been crawling around that field all day. And I don't *do* that."

"It's cheating," said Erica. "Isn't it, Wiggie?"

"I suppose it is," Wiglaf said.

"See, Gwen?" said Erica.

"But it is clever," Wiglaf went on. "If Mordred sees many, *many* lucky clovers, perchance he will not make us wear eels."

"No eels!" everyone around cheered.

Gwen gave Wiglaf a Princess Smile.

Erica gave him a Princess Dirty Look and stomped off.

Gwen wrinkled her nose. "Poor Erica. Is

she always in such a bad mood?"

"No," Wiglaf muttered. He felt awful! Now Erica was mad at him.

He and Angus trudged over to Frypot. They handed him their sack of eels. Then they ran to join the others at the castle steps.

"Look, Headmaster!" Gwen called to Mordred, who was giving Torblad yet another horseshoe to hang up. "We are covered in lucky four-leaf clovers!"

"May they bring us luck!" Mordred cried.

"With so many lucky clovers, we don't need to wear eels, right?" said Gwen.

"Eels!" cried Mordred. "I'd forgotten all about them. Frypot? Give out the eels!"

"Nice going, Gwen," muttered Erica.

Frypot reached into the sack and grabbed an eel. It thrashed wildly as he looped it around Torblad's neck. Torblad burst into tears.

Frypot started toward Gwen with an eel.

"No, thanks," said Gwen. She flashed Frypot a Princess Smile.

"Take it." Frypot held out the eel to her.

"Frypot?" she whispered. "What would it cost me not to wear an eel?"

"I didn't hear that," said Frypot. "Look, here's a little fellow." He put the eel around her neck.

Gwen looked sick to her stomach.

Frypot gave Wiglaf the next eel. It slapped Wiglaf's cheek with its tail. *Smack!*

"Now I'll show you the lucky walk," said Mordred. He bent forward. He began taking baby steps. He thrust his arms out, first one, then the other. He turned his head to the left, then right, left, right, left. He looked to Wiglaf like a badly wounded duck.

Angus groaned. "I can't believe I'm related to him," he said.

"Follow me!" Mordred called.

Wiglaf lined up behind Mordred with the others. He bent over and began taking baby steps. He stuck out one arm. Then the other. He turned his head from side to side. It wasn't easy. Especially with the eel smacking his face.

"Good, good," said Mordred. "Walk this way for the rest of the day, and good luck is sure to follow. Now stop!"

Everyone did, gladly.

"As you walk, you must sing the lucky song," said Mordred. "I shall teach it to you." He burst into song:

> *"Lucky me! Lucky you!*
> *Lucky cow! Lucky moo!*
> *Lucky horse! Lucky neigh!*
> *Lucky night! Lucky day!"*

The song went on and on. It had many lucky verses.

"Chime in!" Mordred cried, starting the song over again.

Softly, the students began to sing:

"Lucky me! Lucky you!
Lucky cow! Lucky moo!"

"Keep singing the lucky song!" said Mordred. "Don't stop! That way, no bad luck can come our way. No dragon can come to DSA. We are lucky! We are safe!"

Wiglaf glanced up. He saw that the horseshoe Torblad had put up over the castle door was hanging by a single nail.

"Sir!" cried Wiglaf. "The horseshoe—"

"No talking, boy!" said Mordred. "Sing!"

The horseshoe swung dangerously above the headmaster's head.

"Lucky you!" Wiglaf sang. *"Lucky horseshoe!"*

The nail popped out of the wall.

Mordred sang: *"Lucky cow! Lucky—"*

CLONK!

The horseshoe fell, hitting the headmaster on his not-so-lucky bonnet.

"MOOOOOooooo..." he sang as his violet eyes crossed, and he fell to the ground, senseless.

Chapter 6

"**M**ordie!" screamed Lobelia. She whipped off his bonnet. The bump on his forehead was quickly swelling to the size of a goose egg.

"Coach Plungett! Sir Mort!" Lobelia called. "Get Mordred to the couch in his office. Stay with him until he comes to."

Sir Mort, in full armor, clanked over to Mordred with Coach Plungett. Groaning and grunting, they picked up the hefty headmaster and carried him into the castle.

Lobelia turned to face the students. "Until Mordred wakes up, I am in charge," she said. "And I say stop singing. Stop doing the lucky walk. And lose the eels."

"HOORAY!" everyone cheered.

Wiglaf led the way to the drawbridge, where they all flung their eels into the moat. They also flung in their lucky bonnets—all but Torblad. They cheered as everything sank down into the slimy moat ooze.

Just then, Wiglaf caught sight of Brother Dave crossing the drawbridge. He had a traveling sack slung over his shoulder.

"Brother Dave!" Wiglaf called out to him. "Wait!"

Brother Dave stopped. Everyone on the bridge gathered around him.

"Where are you going, Bro?" asked Janice.

"I go to meeteth Snagglefahng in the Dark Forest and surrendereth to him," said Brother Dave. "Then he needeth not come to DSA. Farewell, my fond lads and lasses!"

"Wait, please," said Erica. "You must tell

us—why is Snagglefahng coming after you?"

"'Tis a long story," said Brother Dave.

"Tell us, Bro!" cried Janice.

Brother Dave sighed. "All right," he said. "There is time enough. Cometh thou up to the library and hear my sad tale."

The lads huffed and puffed as they ran up the 427 steps to the library. The lasses huffed and puffed and jingled. Soon everyone was sitting down for the story hour Brother Dave had long dreamed of.

The monk went behind the checkout desk. He sat down on a big rock, as his order forbade him to sit on anything comfortable. He held up a book: *The World's 100 Wickedest Dragons* by Sir Heshure Nosalot. He turned its parchment pages, stopping at a picture of a terrible dragon. Smoke poured from a horn on its head. Its eyes were small and mean. Its thin lips were pulled back in a fang-filled grin.

Under the portrait it said: *World's 97th Wickedest Dragon: Snagglefahng.*

"He is scary!" Wiglaf squeaked. His stomach flip-flopped as he stared at the dragon's long, twisted fangs.

On the facing page, Sir Nosalot had written what he knew about Snagglefahng, and he knew a lot.

Full name: *Snagglefahng Suggarlump*
Also known as: *Candylips, Sweetie Pie*
Wife: *You must be joking. Look at him!*
Appearance:
  Scales: Off-off-off-off-off-off-white
  Horn: Spews smoke
  Eyes: Pale blue
  Teeth: FANG-tastic!
Age: *1,465 last hatch-day*
Often Heard Saying: *I'm your worst bitemare!*

Hobby: *Answering mail from his FANG Club*
Loves: *Lollipops, caramels, jelly beans,*
gumdrops, candy corn, etc.
Hates: *Flossing, brushing, regular checkups*
Secret Weakness: *Still a secret*

Brother Dave closed the book and said, "For years, I liveth in the monastery with my fellow Little Brothers of the Peanut Brittle. One dark night, we heareth the beating of wings. We looketh out our window. And there came a dragon most terrible flying down upon us."

"But why would a dragon attack you and your Little Brothers?" asked Wiglaf.

"He cometh for our brittle," said Brother Dave. "'Tis famous the world o'er," he added. "And, except for my own poor batches, it is known to be most tasty."

"What's wrong with your brittle, Bro?" asked Janice.

"'Tis not fit to eat." Brother Dave sighed and went on. "That very morning, I hath badly burned my batch of brittle. My Little Brothers hath placed it on the bottom of the brittle pile. The huge dragon flyeth down and roareth out, *'I am Snagglefahng! Give me your brittle, and no one gets flamed!'* "

"What a bully!" exclaimed Erica.

Brother Dave nodded. "The dragon filleth us all with fright. We cowereth in fear as he gobbleth up all our brittle."

"Mmm, a brittle feast," murmured Angus.

"Snagglefahng eateth his way through our brittle. At last he cometh down to my own poor batch. And when Snagglefahng chompeth down upon my brittle—*Snap! Snap! Snap! Snap!*—he broketh off his four front fangs."

"No kidding?" exclaimed Janice. "Your brittle was that hard?"

Brother Dave nodded sadly.

"You defanged Snagglefahng!" said Erica. "He can't hurt anyone. You're a hero, Brother Dave!"

"Oh, no," said the monk. "For the dragon spouteth fire still. And his claws can rippeth the armor off a knight as easy as they peeleth a grape."

"Brother Dave?" said Wiglaf. "How did Snagglefahng know it was *your* brittle that broketh—I mean, broke—off his fangs?"

"The dragon filleth up with rage," the monk said. "He belloweth out, " 'Who baked that burnt, brick-hard brittle?' "

Gwen gasped. "And you confessed?"

Brother Dave nodded. "I cannot telleth a lie," he said. "And I wanteth to protecteth the other Little Brothers."

"Did he try to flame you, Brother Dave?" asked Erica. "Or rip you with his claws?"

"No," said the monk. "He only pointeth

a claw at me, and growleth that he wouldst be back one day to get his revenge. Then he picketh up his fangs and flyeth away."

Brother Dave sighed and said, "And now I must goeth."

"Hold it, Brother," said Gwen. "Hold it."

Chapter 7

Gwen pulled a magazine from her bag. "I think Snagglefahng is in this month's issue of *WHO'S HOT.*" She flipped through it. "Look, here he is!"

Gwen held up the page for all to see.

"Yiketh!" cried Brother Dave.

Staring out from the page was one very scary dragon. His horn puffed coal black smoke. His eyes shot sparks. He sneered, showing four fang stumps. Under the portrait it said:

World's #1 Wickedest: Snagglefahng

"He went from 97th wickedest to wickedest!" exclaimed Janice. "Way to go!"

Gwen turned the page, and they all read:

FLAMER OF THE MONTH: Snagglefahng!
Snagglefahng Suggarlump was born mean. But when he lost his four front fangs in a freak peanut-brittle accident, he became even meaner. Now he makes up for his lack of scary fangs by flaming first and asking questions later.

Lots of dragons have perfect front fangs. But Snagglefahng has suffered. He's real! He's had to flame and claw his way up to #1 Wicked. That's why he's our Flamer of the Month. Hey, Snaggy, hope you get the guy back—but good!

"Brother Dave!" said Wiglaf. "You cannot go to meet this wicked dragon!"

"Why not?" cried Torblad. "I say let him go! Then the dragon won't come after us!"

"I shalt goeth," said Brother Dave. "But I can stayeth a moment if any of thee wisheth to checketh out a book."

"Oh, gosh!" exclaimed Gwen. She pulled a book from a shelf. "We have this in the palace library at Gargglethorp!" She held the cover face out: *Peanut Brittle Made the Old, Difficult Way with Hours of Standing over a Steaming Hot Cauldron, Stirring Ceaselessly and Sweating Like a Pig.*

"Doest thou now?" Brother Dave beamed. "'Twas written by all the Little Brothers. I helpeth to letter it myself."

"No kidding!" said Janice, leaning over the book.

"I kiddeth you not," said Brother Dave. "My order selleth this book, as well as our brittle, to maketh our meager living."

"My mother, the Queen, would never stand over a hot cauldron," Erica said.

"Mine doesn't either, silly," said Gwen. "We have a palace brittle baker."

Torblad gave a sudden shriek from where

he sat, looking out the library window. All turned to see what ailed him.

"Look! In the sky!" Torblad wailed. "It's the dragon! He's coming! We're doomed!"

Wiglaf ran to the window. Far to the west, he made out a small, dark shape flapping its wings against the sky, still many miles away. Was it truly Snagglefahng?

"I can't believe it!" cried Janice. "First a ghost and now a dragon!"

"To arms!" cried Erica.

"To what?" said Gwen.

Erica rolled her eyes. "It means get your weapon! We must fight Snagglefahng."

"But we have no weapons," Gwen said.

The other princesses nodded.

"We are doomed!" cried Torblad, in case anyone had forgotten. "Doomed!"

"Back to the dorm!" Erica called. "We'll get our swords. Then I'll think of something for the lasses!"

Everyone raced down the 427 stairs from the library. Brother Dave hurried after them.

Back in the Class I dorm room, Wiglaf reached under his cot and pulled out his sword, Surekill. It had been a gift from the wizard Zelnoc. But could he use it? He hated the sight of blood. Even hearing of a bloody battle made him feel sick. Yet he had to help Brother Dave! He stuck Surekill into his belt.

He hurried over to Erica. She had changed into her old DSA uniform.

"How shall we fight this dragon?" he asked her as she stuck her silvery Sir Lancelot look-alike sword into its scabbard.

"Why don't you go ask Gwen?" Erica snapped. "Maybe she'll have a clever idea."

"Come on, Erica," he said, but she was still mad.

Erica called out, "To the Weapons Closet!

Quickly! There's not a minute to lose!"

As everyone thundered down the hallway, Lady Lobelia stuck her head out the headmaster's office door.

"Shhhhh!" she said, putting a finger to her lips. "Don't disturb Mordred. It will be better for everyone if he stays knocked out until Saturday the 14th."

"A wicked dragon is on his way here, Lady Lobelia," Erica said. "We must fight him!"

"St. Patsy's petticoat!" exclaimed Lobelia, and she slammed the door shut.

Erica led the way to the Weapons Closet. She flung it open. "Give out swords, Wiggie," she ordered.

Wiglaf took several. Erica had called him *Wiggie*! Maybe she had forgiven him for taking Gwen's side earlier.

Wiglaf carried the swords to the castle yard. He gave them out to the princesses.

"How do you hold this thing?" Gwen asked Wiglaf. "Is there any way I can get a private lesson?"

"There is no time for a lesson, Gwen," Wiglaf said. "Stick with me at the back of the charge. That way, you and the other princesses will not likely get hurt."

"Stick with me, Gwennie!" Erica mimicked him. "I'll save you!"

Wiglaf felt his face grow warm again. Perhaps Erica had not entirely forgiven him after all.

"Watch me, Gwen," Erica said. "I shall be up front with Janice, leading the charge. Do what I do, and you shall soon get the hang of dragon slaying."

"Of course I shall!" said Gwen fiercely. "I'll take another one of those!" She grabbed a second sword from Wiglaf.

A flapping noise sounded overhead. The dragon was coming closer!

"I'll show you what I learned at Dragon Whackers, Snagglefahng!" Janice cried. She warmed up for battle by swinging her lance wildly over her head.

"And I'll show you what I learned in Knitting Class at Princess Prep!" shouted Gwen. She flashed the tips of her swords together with great skill. Wiglaf thought she looked quite fearsome.

Wiglaf stood between Angus and Baldrick, near the back of the formation. He glanced at Brother Dave. Brother Dave stood beside the castle wall, his hands folded. He looked very worried.

A whistling sound split the air. The dragon was flying in fast. Wiglaf saw a flash of green. A flash of yellow. Then—

THUMP!

The dragon landed in the yard.

Janice called, "CHARGE!"

Class I gave a battle cry: "Yahhhhhhhh!"

Waving their swords, they ran toward the dragon. At the back of the charge, Wiglaf saw the dragon flap its wings and then fold them to its body.

Suddenly, Wiglaf put on a burst of speed. He raced to the front of the formation. He kept going until he was way ahead of the others.

"Stop!" Wiglaf cried as he ran. "Stop! Do not harm this dragon!"

Chapter 8

"**D**RAGON SLAYERS, CHAAARGE!"
cried Janice.

The others kept running after her, waving
their swords and lances in the air.

"Stop!" Wiglaf shouted, still running.

The dragon was hunkered down, its head
hidden beneath its wing.

Wiglaf reached the dragon. He whirled
around and stretched out his arms as he faced
the oncoming mob. "I said STOP!"

Everyone stopped.

"Stand back, Wiglaf," Janice said, "so I can
lop off the dragon's head!"

"Do not lop!" cried Wiglaf. "For this is not
Snagglefahng. This is Worm!"

At the sound of his name, the dragon popped his head out from under his wing. He looked around with yellow eyes that had cherry red centers. He smiled and nuzzled Wiglaf.

"You *know* him, Wiglaf?" said Gwen.

"Worm!" cried Angus and Erica, rushing up to the dragon.

"*Wrrrm comme homme,*" said the dragon. He butted Wiglaf gently with his head.

"Hey, you can really talk now, Worm!" exclaimed Wiglaf.

Janice lowered her lance. "Oh, he's a big baby. This is so cool!"

"He's very cute," said Gwen. "You saved his life, Wiglaf!"

Wiglaf hardly noticed Gwen. How happy he was to see his Worm!

Worm hopped over to Brother Dave. "*Brrrrrr!*" he burbled. "*Brrrr Daaaave!*"

"Worm!" The little monk hugged the dragon. "Thou hath cometh home!"

Worm bounced back to Wiglaf.

"Mommmy!" he purred. *"Wormmm mmmiss Mommmy!"* He rubbed his head on Wiglaf's shoulder.

"He thinks you're his mommy?" said Gwen. "That is so cute!"

Wiglaf smiled. He scratched the dragon behind his ears. Worm was a hundred times bigger than when he had hatched from his purple egg in the Class I dorm. But he would always be Wiglaf's baby dragon. His little pipling.

"The newspaper must have been wrong!" cried Erica suddenly. "Snagglefahng isn't flying to DSA. It was only Worm!"

"Hooray!" everyone cried.

"Good thing I kept on my lucky bonnet!" cried Torblad. "I kept Snagglefahng away!"

"I say we feast," said Angus.

"Hooray!" everyone cried again. They ran toward the banquet table.

But Worm bounced toward them.

"Draaaagon come!" he burbled.

"I know," said Wiglaf happily as he got in line. "Our little dragon has come home."

But Worm shook his head. *"No littttle. Bigggg draaagon. Bigggg!"*

"Thou hath indeed grown big, Worm," said Brother Dave.

"Nott Wrrrm, Brrrr," said Worm. *"Biggg draaaagon coming soooooon!"*

A hush fell on the castle yard.

"Who's coming, Worm?" said Wiglaf.

"Biiggg dragon!" cried Worm. *"Baaaaaaad."* He began bouncing toward the lads and lasses. *"Runnn! Hiiddde!"*

"He's telling us to run and hide!" exclaimed Wiglaf. "Do you think he means Snagglefahng is coming?"

"Who knows?" said Angus grumpily. He gave a last longing look at the banquet table. "You'd better not be playing one of your games, Worm."

Brother Dave hurried over to Worm.

"Telleth me, Worm," he said. "Art this dragon's front fangs brokeneth off?"

"Faaaaangs brrrrken." Worm nodded his head. *"Commmming soooooooon."*

"Unlucky day!" cried Torblad. "We are doomed! Doomed!"

"Never fear! Your teachers are here!" cried the fully armored Sir Mort. He clanked his way down the castle steps.

"Lady Lobelia sent us," said Coach Plungett, coming down the steps after Sir Mort. He, too, wore armor. "We have come to show you how to fight a wicked dra—"

Coach stopped. His mouth hung open. He stared at Worm.

Wiglaf ran forward. "This is not a wicked dragon, sir!" he cried. "This is...this is..." He was at a loss as to how to explain Worm. "He would not hurt a flea, sir!"

"He's cute, isn't he?" added Gwen.

"What are they yapping about, Plungett?" said Sir Mort, whose visor was down over his eyes. "Let's get on with it, shall we?"

"Dragon in the yard, Mort," said Coach. "Not too big. Looks harmless."

"Totally!" said Janice.

"Harmless, eh?" said Sir Mort. "Like a kitten. A fluffy, little kit—"

"We are here!" said Coach, cutting off Sir Mort. "To give you new students a quickie course in dragon stalking and slaying."

Worm hid behind Wiglaf.

"I'm happy to demonstrate!" called Erica. Then she said, "Don't worry, Wormy. No one is going to hurt you."

The princesses lined up with their swords. The rest of Class I stood nearby.

"Stalking a fire-breather is no easy matter, lads," Sir Mort began.

"We're not lads," said Gwen. "We are princesses."

The old knight struggled with his helmet. At last he pushed up the visor and peered out. "So you are!" he exclaimed. "I knew a princess once. No, wait. It was a prince. Only he'd been turned into a toad. Or was it a frog?" He scratched his helmet.

"Sir!" Erica called. "There isn't much time. Snagglefahng is coming. Remember?"

"Snagglefahng, eh?" said Sir Mort. "That dragon bit my shoulder. Gave me a doozy of a wound. Bled like a gusher all night."

"Sir, stop!" cried Wiglaf, gagging at the thought of Sir Mort's nasty wound.

"Remember!" said Sir Mort. "When you stalk, you've got to keep your eye on the dragon. Keep your ear to the ground. Keep your hands at the ready. Keep your mind on the job. And keep your finger out of your nose." He turned to Erica. "Go on, demonstrate."

But Coach Plungett stepped forward just in time. "Thank you for that valuable stalking lesson, Sir Mort," he said.

Gwen said, "*That* was a lesson?"

Wiglaf shrugged. He turned his eyes skyward. The sky looked cloudy...or was it smoky?

"I always warm up my Slaying class with ten laps around the castle yard," Coach Plungett told the new lasses. "Followed by push-ups, sit-ups, and chin-ups. Then, most days, one of the lads throws up." He chuckled at his joke.

Suddenly, the sky grew darker and darker. And yes, Wiglaf definitely smelled smoke.

"Snagglefahng is upon is!" cried Torblad.

"Oh, too bad. Guess we don't have time for a warm-up today," said Coach, speaking very quickly now. "We'll go straight to the basic thrust-and-stab. Hold your sword by the handle. Step forward with your left foot, pull back your right arm, and plunge your sword right into the dragon's gut."

Smoke filled the air now. Wiglaf's eyes stung.

"If you're a lefty," Coach said quickly, "turn it all around. Questions? No? You're ready, ladies!" He began backing toward the castle. "Go get that dragon! Best of luck! Tah-tah!" He gave the princesses two thumbs up. "I'll be watching from inside!" Then he turned and ran into the castle.

Chapter 9

orm bounced over to Wiglaf. *"Runnnn, Mommmmy!"* he cried. *"Hiidddde!"* Then he spread his wings and flew over the castle wall.

"Be safe, Worm!" Wiglaf whispered.

The smoke was thick now. Over the thumping of his terrified heart, Wiglaf heard the whoosh of wings. Not pipling wings. Huge wings. Snagglefahng wings.

THUD!

The ground shuddered as if from an earthquake as the dragon landed.

The smoke began to clear. Slowly, a huge dragon came into view. Snagglefahng stood near a practice dragon. He was ghostly pale. He smiled a fang-filled smile. *Where did those teeth come from?* Wiglaf wondered.

"Line up for battle!" ordered Erica.

All the Class I dragon slayers lined up behind her. Wiglaf was still coughing from the dragon smoke.

Snagglefahng puffed a small cloud of blue smoke from the horn on his head. He squinted at the DSA students before him.

"WHERE ITH BROTHER DAVE?" the dragon lisped. "DRAT THETH FALSE FANGTHS." He reached into his mouth and adjusted his teeth. "I WANT TO THPEAK TO HIM. NOW!"

"Be gone, dragon!" Erica shouted.

"Right!" shouted Wiglaf. "Leave Brother Dave alone!"

Angry black smoke poured from the horn now. "I HAVE WAITED YEARTH," he whined. "I AM THICK OF WAITING!"

The dragon reared up on his hind legs and belched. Flames spurted from his mouth.

"Dragon slayers, get ready," said Erica.

Old Class I students drew their swords. The princesses watched and then did the same.

"We're ready!" shouted Gwen.

"Get set!" cried Erica.

They pointed their swords at the dragon.

"We're set!" shouted Janice.

"Charge!" cried Erica.

They all ran toward the dragon.

Suddenly, a brown-robed figure darted between the dragon and the charging mob.

"Fighteth not!" he cried. "I surrendereth!"

Erica and her troops stopped.

Snagglefahng broke into a grin. "THO, WE MEET AGAIN, LITTLE BROTHER," he said.

"So we do," said Brother Dave calmly.

"Run away, Brother Dave!" Wiglaf shouted. "Now!"

"DON'T LITHEN TO HIM," said Snagglefahng. He waggled a long, curved, sharply pointed claw at the monk. "COME CLOTHER."

Brother Dave walked boldly forward.

In a flash, Snagglefahng hooked the claw under Brother Dave's rope belt.

"THAT'TH BETTER!" cried Snagglefahng as he dangled Brother Dave from his claw.

Wiglaf's heart sank. Poor Brother Dave!

Snagglefahng turned to the future dragon slayers. "THTAY WHERE YOU ARE AND NO ONE GETTH FLAMED."

Swinging from the dragon's claw, Brother Dave said, "I—I never meant to harmeth thee."

"HARMETH THEE?" The dragon's eyes narrowed. "ARE YOU MAKING FUN OF THE WAY I THPEAK?"

"No," said Brother Dave. "Little Brothers of the Peanut Brittle all speaketh like this."

"BRITTLE!" cried Snagglefahng. "YOUR BRITTLE WATH HARD ATH A BRICK!"

"I knoweth," said Brother Dave. "And for

that I am truly sorry."

"WHY THORRY?" Snagglefahng drew the little monk very close to his scaly face.

"Sorry...the brittle...broketh your...fangs!" squeaked the monk.

Wiglaf heard the sound of wings behind him. Then over the castle wall flew Worm! He circled Snagglefahng's head, calling, *"Helllp yoou, Brrrrr! Helllp yoou!"*

Wiglaf watched, horrified, as Worm dove awkwardly at Snagglefahng.

"GET LOTHT, THQUIRT!" cried Snagglefahng. "THITH ITH BETWEEN ME AND BROTHER DAVE." He batted Worm away with a claw, like he was a pesky mosquito.

The blow sent Worm spinning across the yard. He slammed into the wall and slid to the ground. He didn't move.

"Worm!" Wiglaf cried. He found himself racing across the castle yard toward the stunned dragon. "I'm coming, Worm!"

Worm raised his head and rubbed it with a claw. *"Mommmy?"* he whimpered. *"Mommmmy? Wrrmm hass a boo-boo!"*

Chapter 10

Big yellow tears ran down Worm's green cheeks.

Erica and the others ran over to comfort Worm. The dragon wiped his tears with the back of a claw and scrambled to his feet.

"*Wrrrrmmm allll riiiight,*" said Worm. And he began bouncing toward Snagglefahng crying, "*Brrrrr! Wrrrmmm herrrre!*"

"Come back, Worm!" shouted Wiglaf. "You're no match for Snagglefahng!"

Worm bounced back to Wiglaf.

"Let's fight that dragon!" cried Erica. "Form up for battle!"

"COME ON, BROTHER DAVE," said Snagglefahng. "LET'TH GO WHERE WE CAN

THPEAK IN PRIVATE." He spread his giant wings. "THAY THO LONG TO EVERYONE!"

"S—so long!" cried Brother Dave.

Wiglaf's eyes widened. He couldn't let Snagglefahng fly away with Brother Dave! He was only a small dragon-slayer-in-training, but he had to do something!

"Kneel down, Worm," said Wiglaf.

And before he could change his mind, he ran and jumped onto Worm's back. He drew Surekill and threw his other arm around Worm's neck. He held on tight.

"After them!" Wiglaf cried.

"Wait!" cried Gwen. "I want to ride him too."

"Too dangerous," Wiglaf said.

"Not for me!" cried Gwen. "I ride my pony every day!"

Before Wiglaf could say another word, Erica stepped up to Worm.

"This is no pony, Gwen," said Erica.

"Wiglaf is my friend, and I'm going with him to help him!"

Gwen put her hands on her hips. "He's my friend too."

"You may have been queen of the dress-up corner at Pretty Little Princess Preschool, Gwen," Erica said. "But this is Dragon Slayers' Academy. Welcome to my world!"

Erica jumped onto Worm's back, behind Wiglaf. He felt her grip him around the middle. "Let's ride!" she cried.

Worm hopped a few times, testing the weight. Then he began flapping hard, rising unsteadily into the air.

"Good, Worm!" cried Wiglaf. "Higher! You can do it!"

Worm swooped and rolled in the sky. Wiglaf felt dizzy. He tried to steady his gaze. He spotted Snagglefahng circling above them with Brother Dave dangling

from the dragon's claw.

Worm suddenly got the hang of it. He soared upward. Wiglaf clung to his neck for dear life. And Erica clung to Wiglaf. Worm winged his way up until he was high above Snagglefahng. Then he leveled off, flattened his wings to his sides, and dove.

"Aaaaaaiiiiiiiiiyyyy!" cried Wiglaf and Erica as they hurtled downward.

Snagglefahng looked up.

Wiglaf gripped Surekill. He shut his eyes.

"Hey!" Erica cried. "What's the big idea?"

Wiglaf felt her suddenly let go of him. He looked back over his shoulder. No Erica.

"Up here, Wiggie!" she cried.

Erica was clutched in Snagglefahng's other claw. The huge dragon beat his pale wings, treading air. He smiled.

"THURRENDER YET, THQUIRT?" Snagglefahng called to Worm.

Worm answered with a midair flip. Wiglaf clung to his neck, not knowing which way was up or down.

Worm zeroed in again on Snagglefahng.

As they whizzed past the huge dragon, Wiglaf felt himself get yanked off Worm's back. Snagglefahng had hooked him by his tunic!

"Zounds!" cried Wiglaf. "Help!"

"Oh, Wiggie!" cried Erica. "Is this the end?"

"I—I hope not," said Wiglaf.

"Fear not, thou brave hearts," said Brother Dave. "We art not yet goners."

Snagglefahng circled down and dropped his three passengers onto the castle's highest turret. He landed next to them, gripping the turret with big clawed feet.

Wiglaf huddled close to Brother Dave and Erica. He looked down. Everyone in the castle yard looked no bigger than ants. Torblad's shrill little voice floated up to them: "Doom! Doom!"

Snagglefahng poked Brother Dave with a claw. "LITTLE BROTHER—" he began.

But that was as far as he got. For Worm zoomed down, lowered his head, and butted Snagglefahng in the gut—hard!

"OOF!" cried the dragon, clutching his belly. He swayed dangerously, lost his balance, and tumbled off the turret.

Wiglaf braced himself for an awful thud. But he heard only a wild flapping of wings. Then Snagglefahng shot up at a furious speed. He grabbed Worm by his long neck and flew higher into the air.

"Gluuuug!" cried Worm.

"He is a baby!" cried Wiglaf. "Put him down!"

"I WILL," said Snagglefahng. "IF YOU THWEAR TO DO ATH I THAY!"

"I swear!" cried Wiglaf quickly.

"I swear!" added Erica.

"Little Brothers cannot sweareth," said Brother Dave. "But I promiseth!"

Snagglefahng smiled.

Chapter 11

Snagglefahng stuffed Worm under his arm like a toy. He flew to the turret and hunkered down. "CLIMB ON," he said.

Brother Dave, Erica, and Wiglaf helped one another up onto Snagglefahng's wide back. They gripped his scales.

Snagglefahng flew down to the castle yard. He squatted and his passengers dismounted. He put Worm down.

"*Taaaanks,*" said Worm.

The lads and lasses of Class I kept their distance. No teacher came out of the castle.

Wiglaf's heart was still racing. What would happen now?

"THIT DOWN," said Snagglefahng.

Brother Dave and Erica sat on a blue picnic cloth. Wiglaf sat on the grass beside Worm.

Snagglefahng settled himself on the grass.

In the glow of the setting sun, the others in Class I crept closer to the dragon. They sat down too. All waited to hear what the dragon had to say.

"I VOWED TO COME BACK ONE DAY, THEEKING REVENGE," he said.

Brother Dave nodded.

Wiglaf shuddered. He put an arm around Worm.

"BUT I HAVE COME," said the dragon, "THEEKING BRITTLE."

"Brittle?" said Brother Dave. "Very well. I shalt asketh my Little Brothers to baketh you some."

"NO," said Snagglefahng. "I WANT *YOUR* BRITTLE."

"My—my brittle?" said Brother Dave. "The brittle that broketh off thine fangs?"

Snagglefahng nodded. "LOTHING MY FANGTH WATH VERY THAD," he said. "BUT YOUR BRITTLE WATH THUPER. EVER THINTH I TATHTED IT, I HAVE WANTED MORE."

"My brittle?" Brother Dave said again, as if he dared not believe it.

"YOUR BRITTLE," said the dragon. "IT WATH HARD. BUT THE FLAVOR—THUGAR, BURNED JUST THLIGHTLY. MMMMM. IT ITH BY FAR THE BETHT BRITTLE I HAVE EVER HAD."

Brother Dave chuckled. "Thou liketh my brittle!" he said. "Imagine!"

Wiglaf smiled to see the little monk so happy.

"I FLEW HERE," said Snagglefahng, "TO ATHK YOU TO BAKE ME A BATCH OF BRITTLE EVERY WEEK."

"I shalt asketh Frypot if I might useth his kitchen," said Brother Dave. "I canst not think that he wouldst mind. Yes, dragon, I shalt bake thee brittle each and every week."

"And if you thuck—I mean, suck—on the brittle, you won't break your other fangs," Erica pointed out.

"I AM THO HAPPY!" cried Snagglefahng.

Suddenly, Brother Dave frowned. "Waiteth thou, Snagglefahng," he said. "Art thou the world's number-one wickedest dragon?"

Snagglefahng nodded. "YETH, I AM."

"Doest thou flame villages?" asked Brother Dave. "Doest thou rob peasants of their pennies? And others of their gold?"

"I DO," said Snagglefahng. "I AM VERY THUCTHETHFUL."

Brother Dave shook his head sadly. He said, "I canst baketh no brittle for thee if thou art wicked."

"I AM A DRAGON!" cried Snagglefahng. "IT ITH MY JOB TO LOOT AND BURN!"

"Thou must geteth an honest job," said Brother Dave. "With thy flame, thou might helpeth the Little Brothers baketh brittle. Or warmeth the cold huts of peasants on cold winter nights."

"OOOH, REAL WORK!" groaned Snagglefahng.

"Thou couldst let small children climb upon thee for fun," said Brother Dave, "and slideth down thy tail."

"DON'T BE THILLY!" cried Snagglefahng. "OTHER DRAGONTH WOULD THNEER AT ME! THEY WOULD LAUGH!"

"Perhaps," said Brother Dave.

"I WOULD NOT BE LITHTED IN THIR HETHURE NOTHALOT'S NEXT EDITION OF *THE WORLD'TH 100 WICKEDETH DRAGONTH*!" cried Snagglefahng.

"No," agreed Brother Dave. "But thou wouldst have an everlasting supply of my fresh-baked brittle. I shalt leaveth a big bag of brittle on top of Sir Lancelot's Stone in the Dark Forest every Tuesday morn."

The dragon's eyes closed. His nostrils quivered as if smelling brittle. Drool dripped from his lips as he thought how very good it would taste.

Snagglefahng's eyes popped open. "I'LL GET A GOOD JOB," he said.

"Hooray!" cheered everyone.

Erica and Wiglaf leaped to their feet and hugged each other.

"Thanks for jumping on Worm's back with me, Erica," he said. "You are the best friend ever."

"I thought you might pass out up there alone," Erica said. "Especially if you accidentally wounded Snagglefahng, and he started bleeding. Drip...drip...drip. Sticky oozy blood."

"Stop!" cried Wiglaf.

Erica grinned. "Now we're even for the clovers," she said.

Wiglaf smiled, too.

Snagglefahng rose. "MY BITHNETH

HERE IS FINISHED," he said. "I'LL THEE
YOU NEXT TUETHDAY MORNING AT
THIR LANTHELOT'TH THTONE."

"We haveth a date!" cried Brother Dave.

Snagglefahng puffed a cloud of brittle-colored smoke from his horn. Then he spread his wide wings, circled once over the yard, and flew west.

"*Byeee, Snnaggg!*" Worm burbled.

The castle door opened. Lady Lobelia led Mordred outside. The headmaster was back in his cape. But he still had a bump on his forehead the size of a goose egg. He smiled goofily.

"Worm!" said Brother Dave. "Get thee up to the library, quick!"

"Go, Worm!" urged Wiglaf. "Before Mordred sees you!"

"*Okaaaay, Mommmmy,*" burbled Worm. He hopped a few times and took off.

Now the student teachers hurried out of

the castle, carrying torches. They placed them in holders along the castle wall, lighting up the yard.

Coach Plungett and Sir Mort came down the stairs next.

Behind them came Frypot, carrying a tray of steaming hot cherry tarts. He ran over to the feast table and called, "Picnic time! Come and get it or I'll throw it out!"

Everyone—princesses and commoners—lined up at the feast table. Frypot dished out servings of meat pies, bread, cheese, and apples. There was no mention of chopped eel on a toasted loaf.

"Boy, oh boy, oh boy," said Angus as he piled food high on his plate.

Wiglaf did the same.

Janice took her plate and galloped over to where the princesses were sitting.

"We are so lucky to go to DSA!" she said as she sat down. "Isn't this place cool, Gwen?"

All heads turned toward Gwen. She was nibbling on a piece of cheese, holding it Princess Style, with her pinky up. She stopped nibbling and thought for a moment.

"It is," she said at last. "Very cool."

"You know what?" said Wiglaf, lowering his voice so there was no chance that Mordred might hear. "Friday the 13th has turned out to be a very lucky day."

"And it's almost over," added Torblad happily. "Maybe we aren't doomed after all!"

THE END

DSA News

Written by students for students with absolutely no supervision! Vol. I

Get to Know Me!
by Janice Smotherbottom

Hi, guys!

I just transferred to DSA from Dragon Whackers Alternative School. At Dragon Whackers, I was really into sports. I was captain of the Jousting Team, the Fencing Team, and the Whacking Team. I was hoping to do the same here at DSA—but then I found out that DSA didn't have any sports teams. So guess what? I started a DSA Jousting Team! Come and try out for the team! If you don't want to play, we can always use some cheerleaders! DSA has lots of things that Dragon Whackers didn't have, such as Scrubbing Class and scrambled eels for breakfast. Plus DSA is haunted, which is so cool. I'm really glad I transferred to DSA. There is so much happening here!

My Full Name is...
Janice Chainmail Smotherbottom

My Favorite Subject is... *Gym*

My Favorite Food is... *Gum*

My Favorite Riddle is...
Why was Cinderella so bad at sports?
Because her Coach was a pumpkin!

COOKIN' WITH FRYPOT

by Angus du Pangus

Today's column compares how Frypot, our DSA school cook, and his cousin, Halfbake, the chef at Knight's Noble Conservatory, make stew!

SEARED TIPS OF GRYPHON
by Halfbake

Ingredients:

12 pounds finely ground gryphon steak

2 pounds butter

2 t. salt

¹/₂ t. ground black pepper

Sear meat in a frying pan until lightly browned. Add butter, salt, and pepper. Cover pot and simmer for 2 hours or until meat is tender. Enjoy with rice or potatoes.

Serves up to 40 students

BURNED MYSTERY BITS
by Frypot

Stuff to put in:

12 handfuls cut-up meat (eel, boar innards, newt tail, etc.)

6 handfuls lard

moat water as needed to thin

Throw all the stuff into big cauldron, mix it up, and light a fire under it. Boil until suppertime.

Anyone who complains gets seconds.

With enough moat water, it can serve hordes

ASK ERICA!

Advice from Erica von Royale

Dear Erica,

I really want to win the Future Dragon Slayer of the Month Medal. How can I do it?

A Lad from Toenail

Dear Lad,

I work hard to earn this great honor each month. I pay attention in class. I raise my hand to answer questions. And I always volunteer to demonstrate. If you do the same, I'll soon have some big competition. Good luck!

Dear Erica,

Who votes on the Future Dragon Slayer of the Month Medal?

A Lad from Toenail

Dear Lad,

A committee of faculty members and staff. But just who is on the committee is a big secret, so don't think you can butter them up. Again, good luck!

Dear Erica,

I think the whole Future Dragon Slayer of the Month thing is rigged. I'll bet you get it because you're a royal and I'm a commoner.

That Lad Again

Dear Lad,

According to your theory, Princess Gwen of Gargglethorp could get the Future Dragon Slayer Medal next month. Ha ha ha!

Royal or not, I win the contest fair and square.

P.S. I know who you are, Torblad!

Erica:

You wear your FDSOTM medal every single day. Do you wear it on your jammies every night, too?

A Lad from You-Know-Where

Torblad: Go blow your nose!

*** **Have a question for Erica? Write to her in care of the DSA News!** ***

THE DSA SPORTS REPORT

by Charley Marley

The newly formed DSA Jousting team had its first match last Saturday. It was against Knights R Us, who had the advantage of jousting on their home turf, but I'm not saying this is why we lost.

The DSA team traveled to the KRU field in Frypot's ox cart, which had a bad wheel. It was a really rough ride and by the time we got there, all the team members were pretty banged up, but I'm not saying this is why we lost.

The KRU jousters had their own horses. The DSA team shared Frypot's ox. This may, in fact, be why we lost.

FINAL SCORE:

KRU: 873
DSA: 2

Our next game will be this Saturday at Knights Noble Conservatory.

Help Wanted

HARP PLAYER

Accompany part-time balladeer, Professor Pluck, as he sings easy-listenin' favorites such as "Pretty Princess, Please Don't Pout" and "Patsy Picked a Peck of Pickled Peppers."

Contact Professor Pluck

P.S. Umbrella provided.

STABLE MUCKER

Ever mucked out a stable or henhouse or a privy so that it's even semi-clean?

If you answered YES, then YOU may have a future as DSA Stable Mucker!

Perks:

Free room and board!

We don't check references!

We pay you with smiles and pats on the back, not dirty old easy-to-lose coins!

Contact:

Headmaster Mordred, DSA

OVERHEARD IN THE
. . . DINING HALL

by Angus du Pangus

As this reporter strolled from the food line to his table, the following snippets of conversation met his ear:

"What is this stuff?"
"I think it's jellied eel."
"Blaaah!"

"What is lumpen pudding, anyway?"

"To think I used to complain about me mum's cooking!"

"You think Frypot eats what he cooks?"

DSA NEWS

Editor-in-Chief
ERICA VON ROYALE

Reporters
Life Style: ANGUS DU PANGUS
Book Reviews: BRAGWORT
Sports Beat: CHARLEY MARLEY

General Reporting
JANICE SMOTHERBOTTOM
WIGLAF OF PINWICK
Faculty Advisor: SIR MORT

A MATTER OF OPINION

From the Editor's Desk

Lady Lobelia may be a talented fashion designer, but her new DSA lasses' uniforms are not only a joke, BUT also very dangerous.

• The big, floppy bows make it easy for a dragon to hook a lass with a claw.

• The puffy sleeves cut down on speed when drawing a sword.

• It is very hard to stalk with all those pesky bells on the hem ringing and scaring the dragon away.

• The helmets fit over the ears, making it impossible to hear a dragon coming.

I could go on, but I think this is enough evidence that we lasses need to wear the same practical uniforms as the lads.

Lady Lobelia, I beg of you! Use your enormous talents to design gowns for Queens and Dutchesses—but not for DSA lasses.

Fund-Raiser to Be Held

by Charley Marley

Members of the new DSA Jousting Team are having a bake sale next Friday.

"We want to raise money to buy a couple of horses," explained the team captain, Janice Smotherbottom. "With steeds, DSA will be league jousting champs for sure!"

The team also welcomes contributions of any old jousting equipment—helmets, armor, lances, skirts for horses—you may have lying around.

Alumni News

Class of MCCCCLI
Garp of West Upchuckia

After graduating from DSA, Garp moved back in with his parents.

"Life is good," says Garp. "I'm doing exactly what my degree from DSA prepared me for—I sleep until noon and just lie about all day."

Garp would love to hear from others in his graduating class. "Unless they want a loan or for me to help them with anything," Garp adds.

Class of MCCCCLVI
Wulfstan of Vulture Valley

Wulfstan writes:

"I have so many wonderful memories of my years at DSA."

"Unfortunately," Wulfstan's mother adds in a p.s., "ever since Wulfie got conked on the noggin in a sword fight with Harald of Ninnyshire (DSA, class of MCCCCLV) DSA is *all* he can remember."

WHAT'S UP AT THE LIBRARY?

by Wiglaf of Pinwick

The results of Brother Dave's new survey are in!

Last week the DSA librarian asked 53 students at DSA: What is a book?

48 said, "A *what?*"
4 said, "If you don't know, I'm not going to tell you."
Only 1 said, "A written work with pages stitched together along one side and bound in a cover."**

He also asked the same 53 students: How do you get to the DSA library?

23 said, "The *what?*"
14 said, "DSA has a library?"
13 said, "I don't."
3 said, "Go to the South tower, climb 427 steps, and you're there!"

EXCITING NEW LIBRARY BOOKS:

Cheerleading Made Easy
by Ray Teamray

Locked Out!
by Lettice N. Quick

101 Bossy Cow Jokes
by O.U. Laughingstock

The World's Tallest Mountain
by Ken E. Climate

** *(Brother Dave found out that this answer was given by a visitor from Knights R Us, and he had to toss it out.)*